THIS BOOK
BELONGS TO

_____

Feliz Navidad

A Royal Christmas

DISNEP PRESS
Los Angeles • New York

Adapted by **Tom Rogers**

Based on the episode "Navidad," written by **Craig Gerber**

for the series created by **Craig Gerber**

Illustrated by **Mike Wall**

Published by Disney Press, an imprint of Disney Book Group. No part of this book may be reproduced or transmitted in any form or by any means, electronic or mechanical, including photocopying, recording, or by any information storage and retrieval system, without written permission from the publisher. For information address Disney Press, 1101 Flower Street, Glendale, California 91201.

First Hardcover Edition, September 2016
1 3 5 7 9 10 8 6 4 2

ISBN 978-1-4847-4792-6
FAC-038091-16182
Library of Congress Control Number: 2016935475

Printed in the United States of America

For more Disney Press fun, visit www.disneybooks.com

SUSTAINABLE FORESTRY INITIATIVE

Certified Sourcing
www.sfiprogram.org
SFI-00993

This Label Applies to Text Stock Only

Feliz Navidad

A Royal Christmas

DISNEY PRESS

Los Angeles • New York

Elena's Family and Friends

Elena

As the Crown Princess of Avalor, Elena rules the kingdom with help and advice from her family and friends.

Isabel

Elena's little sister is also a princess. She is very smart and creative.

Naomi

Naomi is one of Elena's best friends. Her father is the harbormaster for Avalor City.

Francisco

Elena's grandfather always has a song or a story to share.

Luisa

Elena's grandmother would do anything to protect her family.

Cristina

Cristina is Isabel's best friend. She lives in a village outside Avalor City.

Esteban

Elena's cousin knows all about Avalor's history and traditions.

Doña Paloma

Doña Paloma is the leader of all the shop owners in Avalor City.

"Feliz Navidad, everyone!" Princess Elena calls to her family.

This is Elena's favorite time of year. She especially loves helping her family decorate the castle for the holidays.

"Cristina's here!" shouts Elena's sister, Isabel. She's excited because her best friend has come by to wish her feliz Navidad and to exchange gifts. Isabel has a special **surprise** for Cristina.

Isabel gives Cristina her present: a beautiful engraved box full of art supplies! Isabel designed it to fit onto Cristina's wheelchair.

"It's perfect!" says Cristina.

"Let's make a Navidad piñata," says Isabel. "It's a family tradition."

Cristina's father thanks Elena for being so kind to his family.
"Would you like to come celebrate Navidad in our quiet village?"
he asks.

Elena is honored by his request. But before she can answer . . .

Armando, the head of the castle, pops in. "Um, **Princess Elena**, you have a few visitors. Well, more than a few."

Elena's friends and subjects from all over Avalor have come to invite her to their Navidad celebrations. Naomi says there will be a festival at the harbor; Mateo asks her to join his family in their village; the merchants want Elena to celebrate with them in the town square.

"But our family always spends the holidays together at the castle," says her grandfather, Francisco.

"I wish I could celebrate with all of you. But I can't be five places at once!" says Elena.

Elena comes up with the perfect solution. "Let's go to Castillo Park and celebrate Navidad all together. We can learn each other's holiday songs and traditions!"

Everyone loves this idea.

"We are going to have so much fun!" says Elena.

"I am going to make so much money!" says Doña Paloma, who owns the **biggest** store in town.

She convinces everyone to build holiday floats for a parade to impress Princess Elena. "I can't think of a better way to see who has the best Navidad traditions in Avalor." She tells each group, "If you want to have the best float, you need **more flowers**! **More** candles!

MORE, MORE, MORE!"

They rush to Doña Paloma's store to buy
as many decorations as they can carry.
Before long, she has turned the celebration
into a competition!

In a quiet corner of the park, Isabel and Cristina work on their pretty **piñata** star.

"That looks beautiful!"

The girls turn and see Elena. She's wearing a gorgeous Navidad gown.

"*You* look beautiful!" exclaims Isabel.

Meanwhile, the villagers are getting carried away making their floats **bigger** and **bigger**. **More** fireworks! **More** fountains! MORE, MORE, MORE!

Elena is worried. Navidad is supposed to be fun, not a contest.

FOOSH!

Two floats go out of control.
They crash into each other and set
a Navidad tree on fire!

Thinking fast, Elena leaps onto Naomi's float, which has a **huge fountain** full of water.

"Help me put out the fire!" Elena shouts. They dump the water on the fire—

but that only causes a **flood**,

which carries away the **burning candles**,

which light all the **fireworks**,

which go off with a great **big**

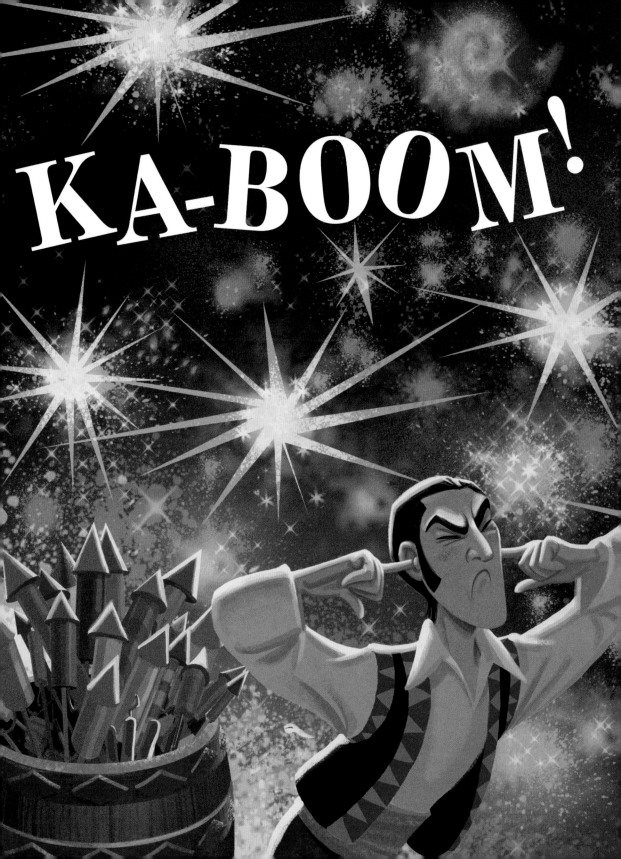

"Oh, no!" shouts Cristina as the fireworks hit their piñata.

It falls to the ground and bursts open. "Our piñata is ruined!" cries Isabel.

The parade is over before it can even begin. The townspeople start to leave. There won't be a celebration after all. Cristina's father starts to take her away.

"Please don't go!" says Isabel. Cristina begs her father to let her stay. But he insists they must go home.

Elena is so disappointed. She wanted everyone to share the joy of Navidad together.

"What happened, Naomi? Why couldn't everyone work together on the parade?" Elena sighs.

"I think I might know where the trouble started," says Naomi.

"You do? Tell me," says Elena.

"It was Doña Paloma's idea."

Elena goes to see Doña Paloma.

"Shouldn't you be at the parade?"
Doña Paloma asks.

"There is no more parade," Elena replies.
"You made everyone so competitive, they
wound up crashing all the floats."

"They could always buy new decorations,"
Doña Paloma suggests.

Elena takes Doña Paloma outside to see the mess. "Navidad isn't a competition, and it isn't about making money!" says Elena. "It's about being with the ones you **love**."

"I can see your point, Elena," Doña Paloma says. "Maybe I did get a little carried away. Is there something I can do now to help?"

Elena sees a guitar hanging in the store window and gets an idea.

Maybe she can help everyone remember

the true spirit of Navidad!

Elena **sings** a song.

It's not all the **gifts,**
The **food,** or **decorations**
But the **spirit** of *love*
That marks this **celebration.**

Elena's beautiful voice draws the townspeople back to the square. Soon they begin to sing along.

Elena leads them on a *parranda*. Together they walk through town, singing the songs of Navidad.

Even Doña Paloma gets in the spirit!

Elena stops to pick up a **special** friend.

Elena leads the *parranda* back to **Avalor Palace**.

You need nothing **more**
Than those you **adore**.
On this **holiday**
Let **love light** the way.

Isabel can't believe her eyes. Cristina's back!
Isabel and Cristina reunite with a huge hug.
"**Feliz Navidad**, Isa," says Elena.
Isabel beams from ear to ear.

This really is the best Navidad ever!

THE END